Chasing Memories

One Family's Journey Through
Alzheimer's

A Fictional Account

Told with Pathos, Humour and
Understanding

Introduction

I was moved to write this story as I wanted to promote awareness of this insidious disease and also to support Alzheimer's Research. I think we all have been touched by the illness to some degree, either knowing a friend or relative with the disease, or maybe even a high profile celebrity. Because it has no boundaries, it affects us all rich or poor, famous or folk just like Nancy.

Whilst working for Age UK as an Intergenerational Projects Officer I was responsible for writing a booklet on Dementia and delivering the content to Primary School children, aged 10 to 11. This informed the youngsters and their teachers of how the disease manifests itself and the importance of early intervention.

I was also privileged to be able to observe a friend's therapy horse at work with Alzheimer's patients and see the incredible results that can be obtained when these animals are employed.

Later I set up my own business, The Nostalgia Road Show and was able to see firsthand how reminiscing via listening to music, sampling different aromas and reading old newspapers and magazines from a bygone era, is so helpful.

For some it instigated lively discussion as we reminisced about life back in the 1940's and 1950's. For others further into their journey and unable to communicate verbally, the music and aromas or horse therapy had a magical touch and gave them moments of pure joy.

So by way of my interaction and close observation of Alzheimer's patients I was able to try to plot a course through the various stages of the illness... However I do believe that the disease may be as unique as the patient, so we will see many different strategies and attitudes when dealing with a diagnosis.

Regarding the end stages of the illness I have had to make an educated guess as to what was really happening in Nancy's world. After all this is a work of fiction, so I leave it to the reader to make up their own mind as to how they would envisage this part of her story.

I leave with you my thanks for reading and please know the proceeds of this sale will go to help find a cure, we are very close, one day we **WILL** beat it!

Patricia Frances Wilkinson April 2024

Chasing Memories

By

Patricia Frances Wilkinson

Chapter 1

Charlie pushed his way through the battered old gate and wandered up the path to Granny's front door. Then opening the letter box he carefully hauled the door key up on its string and unlocked the door, as he so often did on his way home from school.

"I'm here Granny. I've got your shopping," he called out cheerfully as he went in.

He walked along the narrow entrance hall and through to the kitchen where he knew he would find her in front of the old coal fire, although the afternoon was mild for early spring.

He dumped the shopping down on the large central table, then wandered over and took the other rocking chair in front of the range.

Granny looked up from her newspaper where she had been avidly reading the sports page and gave Charlie a warm smile.

"Hello Sunshine, thanks for that, had enough money did you?"

"Yes, thanks."

"And enough for one of those awful brightly coloured lollies full of Z numbers?"

"E numbers, yes thanks Granny, Ma will say I'm hyper when I get in, but I'm not, it's all in the mind that rubbish you know, just thought up by grown-ups to stop us kids having fun."

"As you say dear," she replied vaguely.

"So what did you do today Granny?"

"Oh just the usual my love, David Beckham called around first thing to take me hang gliding , then we had lunch at the Ritz. That Victoria ate hardly anything, poor lamb no wonder she's so slim. Hey ho… Anyway then I just spent the afternoon over at Buck House. The Queen needed a bit of advice on which hats to take on her next tour Down Under and you know how much she relies on my advice."

"Granny…. So what did you really do?" asked Charlie with a huge sigh, rolling his eyes.

"I went to the Day Centre. It was that lovely new driver on the mini bus, Jacob, funny how these old names are coming back in... Well Jake he prefers calls me his Princess, cheeky young whippersnapper, still he means well."

"So who was there, that Mr Williams you fancy? "

"I do not fancy him," she said scandalized," he's just a very interesting gentleman, led a fascinating life, been all over the world he has Charlie, you'd really like him. Anyway no he wasn't, been taken into hospital again, poor man," she said sadly.

"So it was just the usual gang then?"

"Well you could hardly call a group of elderly law abiding citizens a gang, but yes. I sat between Audrey Singleton and Hannah Goodall, we had such a laugh. Oh it's wonderful to get out and see folk Charlie. You've no idea how miserable I get sat in these four walls day after day, if it wasn't for those nice people who run the Day Centre I swear I'd have gone barmy by now."

"Well hang on Granny I visit you don't I? "Charlie said, now looking somewhat dismayed.

"Yes of course you do my lamb. I look forward to your visits all week, and your Mum and Dad, when they can spare the time," she added with a sniff.

"But you see, well it's nice to chat to folk my own age, folk that understand me. Folk that don't look like I'm crazy if I go on about, 'make do and mend' or how I used to enjoy listening to ¹ITMA on the wireless with that Tommy Handley," I wonder what ever happened to him she thought.

"Then there was Workers Playtime," she used to do her housework to that bustling about the place with little Brian and Patricia under foot, "happy days," she sighed lustily.

"Are you OK Granny?"

"Yes my lamb, just thinking back, remembering the old times that's all."

He visibly brightened at that," Do you want to tell me one of your stories about the Olden Days?" he asked eagerly.

She flicked her eyes up to the clock and back to the eager ten year old.

"Well I should like to, but it's time for your tea and you'll have Mum after me if you're late, next time alright my love? "

"OK Granny," he replied jumping up and going across to give her a hug before cheerfully going on his way.

"Laters," he called out at he left, banging the front door behind him.

"Goodbye Sunshine," she said softly, the old house settling around her, the silence almost palpable.

She relaxed back in her chair, now what was it I was about to do before the boy came she thought anxiously. Her old face frowned in concentration, but no, it was gone.

Time was she'd have laughed that off, silly old coot she's have thought you'd forget your head if it wasn't screwed on. But just lately, well over the past few months, certainly since Christmas, she had been… what Charlie called 'losing the plot,' she giggled at the phrase despite her worry, the things that lad came out with.

Anyway she had been losing the plot a lot lately and it was beginning to get on her nerves. Something deep in her brain seemed to have shifted ever so slightly and although she couldn't put her finger on the cause of her anxiety she just knew deep down that something wasn't quite right.

It had all started when she had forgotten her best friend's 80th Birthday. How on earth could she have done that? Goodness she and Susan had been friends since primary school, even though they hadn't met up for nine, no ten years, they were still as close as sisters writing to each other regularly.

It had been Amy, her daughter in law, who had remembered at the eleventh hour and rushed off to the shops buying a special card then posting it first class, with a little note of present to follow.

That had been the start of it and then there had been all the other things since.

Nancy frowned into the fire, then sighed deeply knowing she would have to make her way out to the coal house to replenish the dying coals. Cold for a summer's day she thought idly as she glanced out of the window. Then seeing the new leaves barely formed on the trees she thought goodness girl get a grip it's not summer yet.

When she glanced at the large calendar on the wall she saw it was still March, March the 8th. She had ticked off the date just that morning as she had done every morning for the past few weeks ever since that unfortunate incident with the Day Centre.

She would have sworn on Charlie's life that it had been Wednesday. She had woken early with the light of anticipation in her old blue eyes. Today was Day

Centre day; she must be up by times and have a good strip wash then put on her [2]glad rags before that cheeky young Jake was knocking the door full of his usual blarney.

She had got herself ready in good time, wearing her best jumper and skirt, the pearls Cyril had given her for their 25th Wedding Anniversary and even a dab of that expense French perfume Amy had bought her for Christmas.

She sat in the window waiting for the charity mini bus, with its reassuring bright logo, to pull up by the front of her modest terraced house. She settled down happily to some serious people watching.

She must have been sitting there for nearly an hour when she realised Jake was late, so engrossed was she in watching the passers-by on the busy street. By half past ten she was really beginning to panic, she should be there by now. Being carefully handed down from the mini bus and escorted into the centre by one of those lovely volunteers, the smell of coffee permeating the bright modern building. She should have been exchanging pleasantries with Audrey and Hannah, scanning the room for a sight of Mr Williams, but here she was sitting in her coat still waiting, they had forgotten her. Then her old mouth trembled and she was shocked to feel tears pricking behind her eyes.

"Goodness my girl, behaviour yourself," she said fiercely as she made her way to the phone in the hallway and dialled the charity number.

She had been quite sharp with the young lady at the other end of the line, and she regretted that later. That was another thing she mused now, when did she suddenly get so irritable and short tempered when she never used to be. Patience of a Saint her Cyril used to say lovingly.

Anyway she had harangued the poor girl who simply kept repeating," I'm sorry Mrs Richardson, but it's only Tuesday and the Mornington Day Centre opens on a Wednesday only."

She had rung off feeling stupid and old, although the young lady had tried to make a joke of it saying anyone could get the day wrong. In fact she had done precisely the same thing the other morning waking up expecting a lovely Sunday lie in only to find it was Monday, with work awaiting her.

Nancy had smiled at that, knowing the child was just being kind and had apologized for her attitude then had rung off, sinking down on the hall chair, feeling such a fool.

So now she had the calendar in place and with Amy's help had been through it ringing off all the special dates, anniversaries, birthdays, her doctor's appointments and all the other odds and ends she seemed unable to remember unaided now.

Chapter 2

It was about a week after Charlie's last visit and she was expecting him any day now as he often popped in towards the end of the week with a few odds and ends of shopping if she telephoned Amy with her list.

She had just finished her lunch, when she was startled by somebody knocking loudly at the door and she called out," Key's there as always Sunshine, let yourself in."

When there was no reply bar a further tattoo on the door she pulled herself up from her chair, made her way slowly through the hallway and eventually pulled the door open to a personable young man in some sort of uniform.

"Electricity Madam," he said smiling and flashing a card in front of her.

She peered at the card and then looked up at the handsome youth, "I've left my readers in the kitchen young man, just have to take your word for it."

"I can wait," he said kindly.

"No… no, you look trustworthy enough, so what do you want dear? "

"I'm here just to read your meter Madam."

"I beg your pardon?"

"Your meter, electricity meter, I just need to read the number, for your bill…. You know?" he said more loudly.

Nancy looked surprised," Why no dear I think you have the wrong house I cook on gas you see."

The young man sighed deeply.

"I'm sure you do my love, but you use electricity for other things don't you, your lights for example," he said nodding to where the hall light was casting its faint glow.

She gazed up like she had never seen it before then looked back at the young man, obviously pulling herself together, "Oh of course, silly me and for the telly too."

"That's it," he said his features relaxing into a smile," so may I?"

She stood to one side to let him in and he stood waiting to be directed.

When Nancy didn't move he said in a kindly voice, "So where's the electricity meter then my love, can be anywhere in these old houses."

Nancy felt a stab of panic, where the dickens was the darned thing? Good grief she'd lived in this house for nigh on fifty years, of course she knew where it was … think girl, think!

He looked around him," It's under the stairs maybe?"

Her old face relaxed into a relieved smile and she opened the cupboard, then she went through the usual procedure of pulling out the vacuum, clothes horse, spare torch and various other items of clutter before he was able to gain access to take his reading.

Once he had left she pushed everything untidily back again and then collapsed on the hall chair, tears in her old blue eyes," What's happening to me," she whispered," I really think I'm going barmy…..' I cook with gas,' what must he have thought?"

So life went on, with one day following the next with nothing to choose between them save the revered Day Centre visit and the usual ten minutes with young Charlie when he popped around with her shopping.

Nancy tried to keep to a routine, hell she thought she didn't want to end up like one of those old codger one sees in those BBC documentaries sitting like a cabbage in a Care Home looking vaguely into space. Yes, a good routine was definitely the answer, but just lately Nancy's routine seemed to be sabotaged on a regular basis.

Just the simplest of tasks seemed to take longer, from washing and dressing in the mornings to preparing her simple meals. The main culprit was her memory; she seemed to be going through a phase of misplacing things.

It was just a phase Nancy kept telling herself, everyone had their off days when they misplaced things, but now her off days seemed to be outnumbering her good days. It was such silly things too and she would maybe have laughed about it, if she had someone to share the situation with.

 The day she put her glasses in the fridge… that had been almost funny, but irritating at the time. Then there were darn right silly things like the time she spooned strawberry jam into her cup instead of coffee that had made quite an interesting drink she had reflected later, maybe she would start a new trend.

But there were more embarrassing and worrying things too.

Why only the previous week she had been deep in conversation with Mr Williams, at the Day Centre, when she had forgotten the name of an object, not once but several times. Then after a while he had given her an odd look, made his excuses then wandered off to find a more sensible companion.

Then there had been the time recently, when she couldn't for the life of her remember her daughter's married name. She had the birthday card all ready to post and got as far as Mrs Patricia… In the end she'd had to look up the address in her book, even then she had to go through the whole book before she came across Patterson near the end. Mrs P .Patterson, of course you silly goose she admonished herself, just glad that there was nobody around to witness this latest lapse.

However things really came to a head a few weeks later.

Nancy was out in the back garden feeding the birds. She had topped up the nuts for the Blue-tits, scattered some bread crumbs around on the grass for the ground feeders and was just turning to go in when the next thing she knew she was sprawled flat on her face on the gravel path.

She just lay there for several long minutes totally winded , unable to move, then using all her strength she managed to roll over onto her back, but now felt like one of those black beetles rolling around and unable to right herself.

He face was smarting with pain where it had come into sharp contact with the gravel path and she could feel blood trickling down one knee, but at least it didn't feel like anything was broken.

She called out weakly," Pete… Peter are you there dear?" But in her heart she knew the young man next door would be at work for at least another hour, maybe longer if he called in at the local pub on his way home as he sometimes did.

She must have nodded off because the next thing she was aware of was a nice young man in a peaked cap and dark uniform leaning over her, gently tucking a warm blanket around her.

"It's OK Mrs Richardson," he said with a reassuring smile, "your neighbour phoned us, seems you had a tumble in your garden. So we're just popping you up to hospital for them to check you out, is that alright my love?"

She nodded weakly.

She quite enjoyed the journey in the ambulance, although she was disappointed the siren wasn't on. Then they made a big fuss of her at the other end in the small county hospital with a lovely dark eyed Indian doctor gently examining her.

It was decided that she should stay on the ward overnight.

After supper she was dozing when someone touched her hand and said urgently, "Mum... mum are you OK?"

Her eyes flickered open to see Brian standing there looking totally lost.

She swallowed wondering why her mouth was so dry and then remembered her ordeal out on the path all afternoon.

She finally managed to speak," Yes dear of course I'm alright; just sorry to drag you all the way over here."

Brian sank down on the seat beside the bed, "Oh Mum," he whispered, "your face."

"Well what's wrong with it?" she said stoutly, putting an exploratory hand up and meeting hot swollen skin.

"Don't," he said quickly pulling her hand back and holding it," don't touch, you've just a few grazes from the fall, shouldn't touch them… infection you see?"

"Eh son do I look terrible?"

Brian looked down at the multiple cuts and bruises covering his mother's face, the two fast forming black eyes and quickly pulled himself together.

"No Mum, nothing that won't heal anyway, so what happened?"

Nancy tried to think, she had fed the blue-tits and all the ground feeders, turned back to the house anticipating Countdown on TV and then she was 'down for the count,' she almost chuckled at that, but on glancing back at Brian's anxious stare thought better of it.

"I don't know," she whispered," it just sort of happened, I just fell, no real reason."

Chapter 3

After school the next day Charlie arrived at the hospital and was allowed in to see his gran, the ward sister being a big friend of his Mum who he called Auntie Jenny, although she wasn't really his aunt.

"You are sure Amy, Mum that is, knows you're here aren't you dear? "

"Yes, I'm sure, check if you want," said the youngster offering his phone.

She shook her head, "No that's OK dear, but don't stay too long I think Granny is still a bit confused."

Charlie marched into the ward containing four beds, three of them empty, bar the one containing his gran. He went over, then sat down peering at her sleeping face, now almost black and blue and he gave a little shudder of unease.

Sure he'd seen people beaten up before on videos and cartoons, but this was his gran, this was real.

He sat there studying her tired old face for several minutes before she was finally aware of his presence and opened her eyes.

She beamed at him as soon as she realized who it was," Why my Sunshine what are you doing out here?"

"Got the bus Granny, no probs," he said calmly.

"Well my lovely, good day at school?"

"Yup. So how about you Granny, what happened to you? "

"Oh nothing dear, just a silly little fall," she said quickly, wanting to change the subject.

"So you're OK then, it's not as bad as it looks?" he persisted.

"No dear, I'm fine really."

"So what have you been doing here all day, was it boring?"

She looked back at him her eyes blank for a moment ,then said," Well I'll tell you Charlie I've had simply the worst day and the sooner your father comes and springs me from here the happier I'll be."

Charlie chuckled at that, "You make it sound like prison Granny."

"Umm, well maybe that's what it feels like my lovely. A prisoner of war camp maybe and I've been interrogated by the Gestapo!"

"What are you on about gran?"

She sighed deeply," First of all I had all these wretched tests, blood, x-rays, blood pressure, scans, you name it they checked it."

"I expect they're just being sure you're OK to come home," said Charlie helpfully.

"Yes, well that's the next thing. This young whippersnapper of a doctor came to see me, couldn't have been more than twelve, certainly didn't look like he was out of short pants anyway," she said with a dismissive sniff.

Charlie grinned at that idea.

"Well it wasn't any laughing matter my boy," she said stoutly, "damn cheek of the lad trying to make out I was senile or something."

Charlie looked shocked for a moment, he had never heard Granny swear before, but he recovered quickly.

"What's senile Granny?"

She tapped her head," You know barmy...old and barmy, cheek of the boy!"

"Nancy he says, without a by your leave, Nancy can we do a little quiz together, patronising little sod."

Charlie blinked again at this, what had got into his gran, maybe it was the medication he thought sagely.

"So what was the quiz then?"

"Oh some rubbish, wanted me to take seven from a hundred and keep doing it, well he was flogging a dead horse with that one you know me and sums."

He grinned then," Yup, not your strong point eh Granny?"

"Don't you be cheeky young man," she said, but with a twinkle.

"Then he wanted to know the date, well I told him straight, call himself a doctor and he didn't even know the day of the week , with our lives in his hands? Well I told him that doesn't look too good young man does it?"

Charlie grinned.

"Anyway, I humoured him, told him the date and drew him a clock face, all a waste of time of course. But then we had quite a nice chat afterwards, told him my little joke about helping the Queen out choosing handbags and hats and the like, he laughed at that."

"You and your jokes Gran," he giggled.

"Umm, well so he says you like the Royals then, so who's your favourite?"

"Well I told him Princess Di, so kind and caring."

"Then you know what he said? 'Wasn't it a tragedy'?"

"I said tragedy? What do you mean and he said she was dead! Well that's a terrible thing to say, I mean think of those poor little princes without a Mam, doesn't bear thinking of."

Charlie stared at his gran, "But Granny… "

Just then his auntie Jenny arrived, "I think maybe Granny's getting a bit tired now Charlie, I've just finished my shift and I'll drop you home. I need to chat to your Mum and Dad anyway."

"OK auntie," he leaned over and kissed Nancy.

"See you soon Gran, you will be home this week won't you?"

"Oh yes dear, nothing wrong with your old Gran, I'll see you on Friday as usual," and she waved him off, before sinking back on the pillow feeling weary.

Where did that young doctor get off saying dreadful things like that about Princess Di, she thought as she dozed off, she should report him, really she should.

Chapter 4

Brian helped his mother out of the car and taking her arm walked her up the path then stopped at the door.

"Got your key Mum?"

"The key is on the string Brian."

"Oh Mum how many times do I have to tell you! Anyone could break in and mug you, then rob the place," he said in exasperation.

"Oh stop fussing dear, nobody knows about it except family and Pete next door. Anyway I've nothing worth stealing have I?" With that she pulled the key up, opened the door and marched into the front parlour, Brian being a guest after all.

"I'll put the kettle on Mum," he said shrugging off his anorak and leaving it untidily on the hall chair.

Nancy divested herself of her mac too, then sank down on the sofa and looked happily around at her nick- nacks and the good pink Wilton carpet that matched the floral loose covers on the suite so well, and gave a little sigh of relief.

Then she heard Brian banging about in the kitchen.

"Bring us a biscuit with the tea will you dear," she called out," one of those...in the red wrapper...

fingers...chocolate. Oh Lord what are the wretched things called?"

"Kit-Kat Mum?"

"Yes, of course a Kit Kat in the Duke of Edinburgh tin on the fridge dear."

Brian returned five minutes later bearing a tray with two mugs and a couple of Kit-Kat bars.

"Oh Brian you might have brought plates what are you like!"

"Sorry Mum," he returned with a plate a piece and settled to his tea.

After a while he peered over the rim of his mug at Nancy.

She glanced back, "What?"

"How are you feeling now?"

"Oh alright dear, I'm glad to be out of that place anyway."

"It wasn't so bad, they were kind weren't they?"

"Oh yes, kind enough, that Jenny, your Amy's friend was lovely. More than I can say about that young doctor, hardly in long pants and spouting so much rubbish. Honestly what is the NHS coming to

27

wasting time and money getting kids to ask all these daft questions?"

"Mum he was a Professor, a specialist in Geriatrics, you were lucky to see him."

"There you go again, geriatrics... geriatrics I'm not a geriatric!"

"It only means elderly Mum, there is no offence intended."

"Well there's plenty taken, I may look old Brian, but up here," she said tapping her head," I'm still about twenty-five."

"Yes Mum, so you always say."

There was silence in the room for a while as they ate their Kit-Kats, drank their tea and then Brian finally tried to broach the subject he had been dreading since his interview with Professor Wilde earlier that day.

"You see Mum those tests the Professor did with you are to check out how your brain, well your memory especially is working."

Nancy just stared at him, her mug suspended half way to her mouth," Go on, "she said eventually, her tone icy.

"Well, err," Brian seemed to be having trouble making eye contact and stared hard at a small stain on the bright pink carpet.

He sighed deeply and tried again," Well, it seems that according to the tests you could be in the early stages of dementia... well Alzheimer's actually he seemed to think...although they won't be sure until they've done more tests.

The room suddenly seemed to be deathly silent save for the steady ticking of Mr Richardson's retirement clock on the mantelpiece.

After what seemed an age Nancy finally spoke.

"I think it's time you left now dear, they'll be getting fed up at work, you taking all this time off."

"Mum, did you hear what I said?"

"Of course I heard, I'm not deaf Brian. I'm not stupid either, there is absolutely nothing wrong with me... now off you go, run along dear and I'll see you in a couple of weeks for Amy's birthday."

Brian just sat there and shook his head.

"Look Mum they just want to run a few more tests, then if you do have it, well it will be caught early. They have some wonderful drugs now that really help, well most people anyway, and the sooner you get them the sooner you'll be … what is it you say…all tickerty-boo again," he said with a hopeful smile.

"Put the latch down on the door when you go will you dear, I'm just going up to get changed and maybe have a shower I can still smell that wretched place on my skin."

With that she stood up and after stooping to kiss his cheek made her way slowly upstairs.

She paused by her bedroom door, then after a few minutes she heard the front door bang.

She let out a sigh of relief before entering her room and sinking down on the large old bed.

Then she picked up the wedding photo of her and Cyril from the bedside table and stared lovingly at it.

"Would you believe it love, but they're all saying I'm batty now, some young doctor, even our Brian, eh you'd be so mad at him if you were here wouldn't you lovey."

Then she kissed the photograph and got slowly up to make her way to the bathroom and the comforting warmth of the shower.

When Brian returned home from the office that night Amy came out of the kitchen to greet him.

"Well how did she take it?"

He shrugged off his anorak and put it on the hall stand before making his way into the front room where he slumped down on the sofa.

"Well," said Amy impatiently," you did tell her?"

He nodded, suddenly feeling near to tears for some reason, this was Mum. His Mum, the tower of strength, who had seen him through his O Levels, then the A's and been so proud when he got the place at Nottingham Uni.

Told all her friends, "Eh, our Brian is the first in our family to get to University you know and he's really going to make something of his life."

He'd felt sorry for his Dad then, as though his life amounted to nothing just because he'd come up the hard way, through the ranks, with Rowlands Roofing Company. But he'd worked hard and been their top Sales Manager when he'd retired.

"Brian are you in there?" Amy said sinking down next to him and throwing him an irritated look.

"Oh, sorry dear, Ma… yes I told her, but she… well she just doesn't want to know, says she's fine. "

"Well she would, wouldn't she? Come on Brian she's not been the [3]full shilling for a while now, even our Charlie has noticed."

"Yes well she's old isn't she," said Brian defensively," she's bound to be slowing down a bit, getting forgetful."

Amy sighed, "So you're doing nothing then?"

"What can I do," he spat, suddenly angry," if she doesn't want further tests I can't force her!"

Amy gave a lusty sigh," No I suppose not," then she stood up and wandered off towards the kitchen, "liver and bacon OK?"

"Terrific, thanks love," and he snapped on the Six O'clock News.

Chapter 5

It was the following week when Nancy received the visit from the Social Worker.

The door knocker had gone, mid-morning when Nancy had been enthralled by a programme about buying holiday homes abroad so nearly didn't answer it. However when the knocking persisted and then a high pitched female voice called through the letter box," Mrs Richardson, are you there my dear?" well she thought she'd better see who it was.

She walked slowly to the door and was met by an eager looking young woman in one of those long, hippy looking dresses, a knitted bag across her shoulder together with an earnest look in her eyes.

So what have we got here, Nancy thought at once, but smiled anyway," "Yes? "

"Oh hello dear, my name is Cathy Ballinger, Social Services," she said with a little smile and flashing an ID card on a cord around her neck.

"Well," said Nancy, now slightly less welcoming, "yes? "

"I wonder if I might come in, just for a little chat, nothing heavy," she said with a girlish giggle.

Nancy sighed and stood to one side," You'd better come in then."

Cathy came and took a seat in the front parlour while Nancy reluctantly turned the sound down on the TV. But she left the picture on, of an idyllic villa in Portugal, which she kept glancing at, before finally giving herself up to the presence of this rather untidy young woman.

"So Mrs Richardson, or may I call you Nancy?"

Nancy , smiled and bowed her head graciously, giving a small nod of assent.

"Well then Nancy I'm just here to see how you're coping really dear after that nasty fall?"

"I'm fine thank you," said Nancy throwing her an icy stare," so why do you ask?"

"Well It's my job dear and there has been some err... concern as to your wellbeing?"

"Oh really," she replied looking even more annoyed.

"Umm, your daughter in law contacted us actually. It seems she is worried about you, how you're coping in general?"

Nancy sighed getting slightly weary with the singsong way the young woman spoke with a question mark punctuating every comment.

"I don't know what's come over our Amy sticking her nose in this way really I don't! Cope... cope what does she mean I can't cope?"

"Well dear with your mobility, it might help to have a few aids around the place, a Zimmer for instance, grab rails in the bathroom, maybe even a stair lift? But of course if you would like a full assessment I can send one of the team out?"

"Grab rails...a Zimmer!" cried Nancy her voice rising to a shrill crescendo.

"Well yes dear all useful aids for the senior citizen, better safe than sorry?"

"Look I've had just about enough of this," said Nancy completely losing her patience now," I think you'd better go!"

"Oh... well yes of course?"

"For goodness sake," muttered Nancy under her breath, the woman really getting on her nerves now.

As soon as she left she picked up the phone to call Amy and Brian's landline number and after a moment her daughter in law's posh telephone voice came on the line ,"4351 who's calling please?"

"Amy what the hell are you playing at sending that cretin from the Social Services around yattering on about Zimmer frames and stair lifts?"

"Mum is that you?"

"Well who do you damn well think it is girl!"

"Well it doesn't sound like you, goodness Mum you never swear what on earth has got into you? "

"Well I'll tell you exactly what's got into me; I'm just plain fed up with people meddling in my life, what with young doctors asking me tom fool questions, declaring me barmy. Then some jumped up girl banging the door and wanting to turn the place into a glorified rest home… It's not good enough our Amy and I'd thank you not to interfere again," and she slammed the phone down.

"Well that told her," she said triumphantly, before going back to the end of 'A Place in the Sun.'

Chapter 6

"OK settle down Year 6... All eyes this way... I'm waiting Jeffery Potts...thank you."

"Now guys we have some very special guests in school this afternoon, they are from a Charity for the Elderly and they're going to talk to you about dementia. Ladies welcome," said Charlie's teacher Mr Gordon.

Charlie watched with interest as the two ladies introduced themselves, one with white hair and a twinkle in her eyes, was obviously no stranger to dealing with school children, he thought, as he watched the practiced way she addressed the class. She looked kindly but firm, a knowing glint in her eye, ready to deal with any trouble makers.

The other lady was younger with long dark hair and a funny accent .... Geordie, that was it, she spoke Geordie .He found the northern twang very agreeable, but before long he was no longer listening to the accent, but to what she was actually saying.

The older lady had set the ball rolling by asking if anyone knew what the word dementia meant, then that clever clogs of a swot Brian Jenkins had put his hand up and said, "Is it that thing where old folks forget things, like big time Miss?"

The lady had smiled and said that was certainly could be one of the symptoms, then had gone on to show a Power Point presentation explaining exactly what it was all about, along with the nice Geordie lady who seemed to be a real expert. She ran a self-help group for people with the illness and was full of interesting stories.

At first Charlie watched with detached interest. The very fact that he was missing a cross country run was a bonus. Especially as it was now tipping down with rain outside.

However as the afternoon wore on his relaxed countenance gradually changed to one of concern and then outright apprehension and finally distress as it gradually dawned on him that the case history they were describing could have been Granny.

It was when they went on to explain about the gradual decline from being absent minded to the final scenario when the patient sometimes forgot the names of loved ones, heck couldn't even recognise loved ones, and were unable to do anything for themselves anymore that he had begun to feel very distressed.

If Granny really had this thing well would she end up not knowing him or Mum and Dad? Not calling him her Sunshine anymore. Not chatting away about her make believe day, when she always tried to think of something outrageous to make him laugh.

Once some booklets had been given out the class were all divided into groups and settled down to work on a project around the recent lesson. Charlie became detached and upset, refusing to take part, kicking the table leg irritably.

Mr Gordon noticed at once and Charlie could see he was advancing on him, about to bawl him out for misbehaving, he guessed. Then the white haired lady intervened and after a whispered conversation came over instead.

She hunkered down beside him and gave him a kind smile," Charlie isn't it?"

He just nodded, feeling tearful, wondering if he was in trouble, but she merely gestured for him to follow her to a quiet place at the back of the classroom and sat down next to him.

After a while she said softly, "When I asked if anyone had somebody they knew with the disease I don't think you put your hand up, but I get the feeling you're a bit upset?"

He swallowed hard but said nothing for a while, just sat looking down at the floor. But when the lady seemed happy to just sit quietly with him, he finally opened up and told her all about Granny. About her losing the plot and then having that fall, about thinking Princess Di was still alive and all the other things that had happened since Christmas.

"I see," said the white haired lady seriously," and I imagine you're a bit upset because you think you're Granny may have dementia?"

He just nodded dumbly her kindness making him feel even more tearful.

Anyway she explained that it was often difficult to make a proper diagnosis so if the family were worried then they should try and get his Gran to go for the tests as early treatment often helped.

"Why not show Mum and Dad your booklet, talk it over with them, then you can all decide what's for the best," she said smiling at him.

Charlie nodded, of course Mum and Dad would know what to do, the relief was tremendous.

"Thank you Miss," he said, suddenly feeling more cheerful. Then the bell went and he was off out the door, pushing and scrapping with his mates as they made for home.

It was later that evening after his father had switched off the BBC News that he broached the subject. Wandering over to sit on the arm of his Dad's chair he displayed the 'What is Dementia ?' booklet.

"What have you got there, Charlie boy?" Brian asked genially.

Charlie explained, said what the nice lady had said and passed over the booklet.

Brian and Amy, who had just entered bearing a tray of tea, exchanged an anxious glance, before she poured out the drinks. Then she took the brightly coloured booklet from Brian and flicked through the pages.

"So do you think she's got it Dad?" Charlie asked again, waiting patiently for a reply.

Brian cleared his throat and looked uncomfortable.

"Well she's old you know son, the elderly do get a bit... well strange, fanciful, forget things and the like."

"Oh for goodness sake Brian, be honest with the boy," said Amy, suddenly angry.

"He's ten years old, not a baby, he's going to have to face it sooner or later and so are you."

"So I'm right then," he asked turning troubled eyes to his father," Gran has got it and she's going to forget us... forget me?" he asked in a small voice.

Then his Mum took pity on him and patting the seat beside her on the sofa gave him a comforting smile as he bounced down next to her.

"We don't know for sure sweetheart, but the doctor at the hospital seems to think so, but she needs more tests to be certain and Gran... well she's being a bit stubborn about it all."

Charlie considered this and then turned back to the booklet," but it says here early ineter... intra... "

"Intervention?"

"Yeah, that's it, early intervention, that's like treatment, well that can help people sometimes, might mean she doesn't get ill too fast... sort of slows it down sometimes Miss said."

"Umm," said his Dad," but you try telling her that son."

"OK," said Charlie beaming," I'll go round after school tomorrow."

Amy and Brian exchanged a look over his head, and then Amy shrugged, "It can't do any harm I suppose."

"Well, I don't know son, she may get really angry."

Charlie just grinned at his father," No she won't Dad she never gets mad at me; she says I'm her little ray of sunshine."

Brian shook his head sadly but decided to keep quiet, maybe the boy was right, and maybe she would listen to him.

"What! What did you say young man?"

"Just that maybe you should listen to that doctor Gran, this lady at school from this Age…something charity, told me all about Alzheimer's and if you might …sort of have it a tiny bit... then well it makes sense to see the doctor," said Charlie looking close to tears.

"So who is this lady from school, another do- gooder poking her nose in I expect!"

"No Granny she wasn't really, she was just trying to help, honestly."

"Well I don't need any help and if you're another one who thinks I've joined the barmy army you can hop it too," she said harshly.

Charlie looked red in the face, "I don't I think that, it's just..." he stammered.

"Go on, clear off," she shouted leaning forwards and picking up her walking stick and waving it menacingly at him.

Charlie was up, across the room and out of the door like a bullet and she heard the front door slam loudly a second later.

It was very quiet after he left and she sat there trembling, before sinking her head in her hands and starting to cry quietly.

It was probably no more than a few minutes later when there was a tremendous hammering on the front door.

"Oh whatever next," she sighed before pulling herself up out of her chair. Then whisking a hanky from up her sleeve she gave her eyes a cursory wipe before shuffling off to answer the continued loud banging.

"Alright, alright…I'm coming," she called out, then more quietly," so where's the blooming fire?"

She heaved the door open and was almost trampled aside by a distraught looking young man.

"He just ran out…right in front of me…I couldn't do anything!"

"Pardon me?"

"Never mind, do you have a phone…battery's dead," he said pushing a mobile in her face.

Nancy just stared at him looking bewildered, wondering if this was some sort of scam.

The dishevelled, dark haired young man took a deep breath and tried again.

Loudly and slowly, enunciating each word he said," There has been an accident, just outside and I need to phone an ambulance, please may I use your telephone?"

So that was it she thought, not a scam after all then.

"Of course." she said briskly," you only had to ask," and gestured to the phone on the hallstand.

Whilst he rang 999 she shuffled out onto the porch, leaning heavily on her stick and peering out at a small crowd who had gathered just near the corner of the road a few yards away.

Then her inquisitiveness got the better of her and she started off down the road to get a closer look.

As she approached the small crowd seemed to peel back allowing her to see the small crumpled body lying on the road, partially covered by a bystander's coat. The young lady owner of the coat was kneeling down beside him talking quietly, trying to get a response. But the deathly pale child was unconscious.

Then Nancy saw Charlie's thatch of white blond hair and the top of his Star Wars sweatshirt, just showing above the bystanders coat….and the world started to spin, "Charlie, oh Charlie," she whispered.

Chapter 7

Brian held his mother's hand and smiled patiently at her.

"Really Mum, he's absolutely fine, thank God," he added.

" It seems that the young driver was really on the ball, managed to stop even though that little rascal ran right out without looking," he said shaking his head in disbelief, "he's ten for goodness sake not three...should know better."

"You're sure," muttered Nancy yet again, "you're sure he's OK?"

"Absolutely, a glancing blow was what the doctor said, just keeping him in as a precaution to check there's no complications after him being knocked out. But he should be home first thing tomorrow, so stop your fretting will you?"

"I'll try our Brian, but I can't help but think this was all my fault. I should never have got so cross with the lad, eh...he was only trying to help I know that."

"Ah," said Brian light dawning, "so he broached the prickly subject of the dementia lesson he had in school did he?"

She nodded," Eh our Brian I was that cross, I could spit, but now well it all seems so silly making such a fuss, when the little chap could have been…"

"Mum, please he wasn't killed… there was hardly a mark on him, so pull yourself together, let's say no more about it, alright?"

"Alright, but Brian…"

"Yes?"

"Make that doctor's appointment for me will you dear, maybe it wouldn't hurt just to get myself checked out," she said quietly.

Then rallying threw him a hard look, "Prove there's nothing wrong once and for all!"

0000000

All that had been nearly twelve months ago she reflected as she looked around her neat tidy room in the Golden Years Rest Home…

Home she thought sadly, it was no more like a home than the cottage hospital had been. OK they dressed the place up as a home from home. All her old bits and bobs around her…well those that would fit the small sitting room cum kitchen and bedroom anyway.

She was lucky so everyone said. Lucky that Cyril had invested wisely, for a rainy day and she could afford the up market home. Well it was raining to the extent that she'd need to build an Ark she reflected now...chuckling a little at her joke for a moment. Oh yes good old Cyril, she could at least go potty in comfort she thought.

It had been the shock of poor little Charlie's accident that had been the catalyst for everything she reflected. She had been so relieved when he had visited her a few days later, proudly showing her his bruises and declaring he was the talk of the school yard after his accident.

"Everyone thinks it's so cool to be run over that way. It's the kind of thing that happens to Superman!"

"Well you haven't got any superpowers my Sunshine and don't you forget it," she said holding him close..."No more running off that way Charlie."

"And no more waving that stick at me either," said Charlie firmly.

"Never my lovely, never I promise you."

"And you will see that Doctor, get all checked out?"

"I promised didn't I and when did your old Granny ever break a promise eh?"

So yes, that was what had scuppered her...no backing out. No reprieve...no future.

Although there was one of course, a future of sorts that is. Maybe not what she had envisaged, but ' different could still be OK...once one got used to it,' she had said, as she sat back in her familiar rocker, now looking so out of place in the Golden Years Rest Home.

Once the diagnosis had been made everyone said she must move in with son Brian, Amy and young Charlie.

Well she knew right from the off Amy was no happier with the arrangement than she was. It was necessary; even she could see that. But being stubborn she had refused.

She had stayed in her home for several weeks after the initial diagnosis and then some things happened that made life in her beloved home impossible.

Firstly there was the food poisoning.

Well she'd blamed that squarely on Mrs Singh from the corner shop. Even after the powers that be had issued the shop with a clean bill of health saying it was one of the cleanest corner shops in the district.

"Well then they shouldn't make those sell by dates so darned faint," she had protested later. "How's a body to read them I'd like to know?"

Hot on the heels of the food poisoning came another fall in the garden. But as luck would have it Pete, from next door, was around with it being a Saturday afternoon. He'd heard the crash and came running round. This time however she'd sprained her wrist, but still refused to stay at Brian's place.

"I managed all through the blitz, working in the munitions when I was barely out of school. Hardly anything decent to eat, with incendiary bombs landing right left and centre! So I don't think a little thing like this is going to hold me back do you?" he'd asked belligerently.

But the final nail in the coffin as she thought of it was the house fire.

It was September, not really cold enough for a fire, but she was chilly and lit it anyway, then forgot about it. She'd left the damper open on the old range and kindling in the hearth before going off upstairs for a bath. Then she'd felt so drowsy she decided on an early night.

It must have been about three in the morning when she was awoken by the sound of the fire alarm going off...and what seemed like just minutes later the noise of the fire-engine siren...the blue light flickering on her bedroom ceiling.

Then all was mayhem, shouting...the sound of the front door being smashed in and then heavy boots thundering up the stairs. Followed by a cheery young chap whisking her up in his arms and carrying her down a ladder that mysteriously seemed to be beneath her bedroom window. Like eloping she had giggled as the handsome young man held her close telling her not to worry, she'd soon be safe and sound.

Later she had wondered at that. Why hadn't she been terrified? But there again it had all happened so quickly she barely had time, 'Soon be safe and sound' he had said.

But of course she wasn't. Nancy was never to feel truly safe again. In her own bed, in her own home, everything was about to change.

She moved in with Brian, Amy and Charlie as soon as she was released from hospital a week later. She still had a cough and shortness of breath, but they needed the bed, so off she went.

Right from the offset she knew she was there under sufferance. Amy was used to her own time and space during the day and didn't relish spending it with her 'dotty' mother in law...as she referred to her when in the company of her golfing friends.

At first Nancy made an effort. Tried to be interested in the latest soaps and boy bands Amy seemed to favour, although she thought it rather bizarre a forty something ogling all those young boys. What was wrong with folk like Perry Como, and that lovely Russ Conway, she had asked.

"She's living in the past," said Amy later that night, when Nancy was finally in bed, squeezed into the spare room along with the long redundant exercise bike and some of Brian's prized [4]Dinky cars.

"Well she will be won't she," said Brian somewhat acerbically for him, "she's got Alzheimer's. "

"Precisely," said Amy with a snake like smile," and that's why she really needs specialist treatment at one of those Homes. She can afford it, you're always banging on about how parsimonious your old Dad was looking to the future, to a rainy day. Well it's here Brian. In a deluge, go and sort it out for goodness sake...before she drives me crazy too."

And so it was that out of several of the available 'Homes' Nancy finally chose The Golden Years. Well at least she had a choice she said to herself. She hadn't just been pushed into someplace, out of sight out of mind.

This one was a mere two miles from Buttercup Close where Brian and family resided on a 'Georgian estate, three bed luxury detached near all local amenities'.

Well they might be nearby on paper Nancy mused but as far as accessibility from the Golden Years Home they may have been light years away. Even with the best will in the world the two miles or so to the newsagents and pub was too far for even the fittest resident, let alone Nancy who was not fully recovered from the 'fire adventure' as she termed it.

Day one was like the first day at school.... and things weren't about to get better anytime soon. Like school, she had been introduced to her teachers, the care staff, and other pupils... the other residents. It seemed they tended to congregate in the communal lounge every afternoon for tea and cakes. Well bugger that for a game of soldiers Nancy thought after the first time. Oh yes one or two had made an effort, under the watchful eye of Matron, but the rest? It was just as cliquey as school had been she surmised. All with their little gangs of which she was not a member, and doubtless never would be asked to join.

However unlike school she didn't have to mix with them. So she spent the next few weeks in what she called solitary confinement. She'd got her friends, Audrey and Hannah from the Day Centre and of course Mr Williams, if they ever visited which they only did a few times.

But everyone else down her road, her old neighbours were either dead or moved away. Likewise the contacts she'd made at the school gate when Brian and Patricia were small. She'd never felt the need for friends to be honest, happy in her own company. Just her and Cyril, they were the perfect partnership.

But now, now with this bombshell of her deteriorating mind it would be nice...easier like, to share things with an old and trusted friend. Of course there was her best friend Susan. But they only corresponded now and it was difficult to put in words. In fact Nancy hadn't really come to grips with it herself to be honest. Something that would rob her of all her dearest memories... of her whole life? It hardly seemed possible.

So one day ran into another and she got into her own little routine. Routines were good, she was sure someone had said that. Was it that young Doctor from the hospital, or possibly Brian? She couldn't remember... what the hell. But she'd had to start a whole new regime of things to fill her hours. No longer could she go out into her little back garden to feed the birds. She'd tried to scatter a few crumbs in the large, picture pretty grounds of the home. However the gardener had chastised her saying it would encourage rats. So she had trudged back indoors, keeping her eyes down lest she should have eye contact with one of the other 'inmates' as she thought of her neighbours.

Back in the relative safety of her room she read her Yours magazine from cover to cover and then it was time to make a scratch lunch and settle down with those [5]Loose Women on the telly. Oh they were scallywags the lot of them, but at least they had a bit of life about them. Then she switched over for Doctors. That programme made her laugh. The way those doctor's took their patients so seriously, well of course it was fiction...but even so? All those home visits they did for a start. Good grief you had to be practically at death's door before anyone from her Practice would deign to visit. They just said dial 111 out of hours and then 999 if it was an emergency! Well it hadn't been that way in the old days she reflected. That nice Doctor Harrison had been there like a shot if one of the kiddies was ill. Mumps, Measles, Chicken Pox they'd had it all she chuckled. No jabs for everything back then and the doctors earned their money too.

Then she would negotiate her way through the minefield of reality TV shows, through soaps and various dramas until it was time to go 'up the wooden hill to bedfordshire', as she'd said to Patricia and Brian when they were small. Well no staircase here of course, just a few paces from the sitting room to the bedroom next door. And there she would lie hour after hour, unable to sleep, her mind going round and round like young Charlie's hamster on his wheel. The same thoughts...why...why me... and what would happen next?

Chapter 8

The days turned into weeks and the weeks into months and nothing changed for Nancy. Except maybe she became more and more lonely and introspective. And if she was honest she had less of a grip on life. That funny feeling that something deep inside her brain had shifted was even more prevalent, although she couldn't have explained exactly what it was.

A feeling of anxiety...foreboding, almost as though she was all at sea. Helpless, she mused in her more aware moments.

When she forgot things, which she frequently did now, like the name of an everyday object or of a relative or old friend, her mind seemed to go what she called fuzzy. Like a white mist had gathered and was hiding the thing she was desperately trying to recall. Then the overwhelming relief when she finally called it to mind, or more frequently the increased anxiety when she could not.

She missed the day to day routine she'd had at her old home, number 45. The cheerful postman who was always happy to stop for a gossip, even if all he was delivering were circulars. Or begging letters for those poor little abused kiddies or homeless puppies and kittens or those badly treated donkeys...it was endless. Postie had told her not to get upset, you couldn't save the world but even so she felt so guilty when they were consigned to the recycle bin.

Then there was young Pete next door. He was always up for a good gossip session over the garden fence. In the summertime anyway when he'd be sitting out, beer in hand, cricket on that little tinny radio of his. Even when she didn't see him for weeks on end it was comforting knowing there was someone there, just beyond the party wall.

Here there was a Mister Smith on one side of her little [6]flat, who was even more of a recluse than she was and someone called Gloria on the other. She was rather loud and wore way too much makeup, so Nancy thought, and seemed to have a liking for gin. That is if the communal recycle bin at the end of their corridor could be believed. Well they certainly weren't her empties and she very much doubted they were Mister Smith's either. So no, she reckoned Gloria was on far too intimate terms with Mr Gordon's gin.

Oh how she missed Hannah, Audrey and Mister Williams from the Day Centre. That rascal driver Jake and his silver tongue too. But it seemed now she had moved she was out of the catchment area for the bus. Even the service bus only ran every couple of hours and put her off way past the Day Centre. It was too bad she had fumed. She'd really lost her temper when that had happened, which wasn't like her at all. She sometimes wondered if dear Cyril would recognise this angry frustrated woman she had turned into. Wednesday was now just the same as every other day and she had nothing to look forward to. Except for visits from the family of course, but they were few and far between.

Although young Charlie could have caught a bus and visited occasionally, Amy had vetoed it. Ever since Charlie's 'brush with death' Amy had been much more protective of him, even walking him to school for a few weeks, much to his chagrin. Brian finally put a stop to that saying she'd turn the boy into a sissy mollycoddling him that way. So now he walked alone, well with his mates and had to go straight home after school. The possibility of going to see his beloved Granny shot down in flames before he could even start a good argument for his case.

"I said no Charles and that's what I mean...so don't ask again!" Amy had lambasted him.

Being called by his given name was always a sure fire sign Mum meant business so he backed off. Until the school holidays came around and he asked again.

"For goodness sake cut the kid some slack," said Brian irritably. "He's eleven now Amy and off to secondary school next term, you can't keep him wrapped up in cotton wool all his life!"

When Charlie arrived the following morning Matron directed him to Granny's room. Heck he thought it was so long since he'd seen her he'd clean forgotten how to get to her room in the overheated warren of corridors.

He finally found his way to number Three A on corridor Honeysuckle and knocked loudly on the door. He could hear the strains of the TV and the 'This Morning' theme tune through the door, but that was all. No movement or sound of anyone responding to his knocking. Maybe she was in the loo, he thought so he waited and then tried again, but nothing.

He was just about to turn away and look for help from that Matron woman when the door was opened a crack and Granny was peering out. She looked at him with dead eyes, not recognising the little blond child in the Star Wars sweatshirt.

"Yes?" she said blankly, thinking he was maybe collecting for something. A sponsored walk or swim? Darned kids all wanting to be sponsored for something these day she thought idly.

"It's me...Charlie," the youngster said peering up at her through his blond fringe.

When she still didn't react he said," Charlie...your grandson Granny...it's me can't you see?" He asked his voice rising into a crescendo of fear and shock...didn't Granny know him anymore?

She opened the door wider and peered down at him. Then something in the back of her brain seemed to click.

"Charlie...my Charlie! Well goodness me what are you doing standing out there boy? Come in, come in," she cried grabbing him firmly by the shoulder and propelling him inside.

He barely recognised her. She was so thin and kind of shabby looking too he had to admit.

She had something like a soup stain down the front of her home knitted jersey and her hair didn't look right either. The perm she had worn all his life seemed to have grown out and now her white hair hung lankly around her sunken cheeks.

"Granny are you OK?" he asked.

"Fair to middling my Sunshine," she said bravely. "So where did you spring from? Is uh...you know, what's his name... your Dad... is he with you?"

Charlie shook his head, "Nope, he's at work of course, I came on the bus on my own Granny."

"Well goodness me," she said as she propelled him to a seat, "all that way on your own you say Charlie?"

"Heck yes I'm eleven now Granny, practically grown up. Don't you remember, you came to my party? You said I was a real young man now."

She looked nonplussed for a moment and then said," Well of course I remember," and sniffed angrily, "I'm not completely barmy you know boy! "

"I never said...I didn't mean..." stuttered Charlie, unused to this strange angry, skinny woman. Where was his cheery rolly poly Granny?

She recovered her temper quickly though and smiled at him, "Well how are you and your father...Brian?" he asked with a huge smile...of course it was Brian.

"He's fine said he'd visit really soon," Charlie said remembering the quick exchange with his father as he rushed off for work that morning, "Well when I can," he'd amended.

Nancy nodded, but didn't comment and just smiled to herself. Christmas it would be or maybe her birthday?

"So what did you do today then Granny?" Charlie asked hoping for the familiarity of their usual little game. Maybe she'd had a visit to Buck House, or afternoon tea with her favourite singer Russell Watson? But no, there was not a glimmer of the old humour. She seemed to be thinking hard.

"I've just had the usual routine my Sunshine. Although I did go for a walk, um last week...maybe the week before? When we had that nice sunny spell?"

"Did you go somewhere nice Granny?" he asked politely.

"Just in the garden, the grounds they call it posh like," she said pulling a little face. "There's a lake you know, out past that high hedge. I wanted to get close but there's a um... a fence...one of those nasty ones...metal?"

"Was it an electric one?" Charlie hazarded.

"No...Spiky...nasty..."

64

"Oh barbed-wire?"

"Yes that's it barbed-wire but I just couldn't get through it though."

"But why did you want to Granny?"

She focused on him then, "Why to see how deep it was how cold the water too. It looks really pretty, but I imagine it's cold...lakes are you know."

"Well you don't want to get too close, you could fall in Granny, that's why the fence is there," he said sagely. "You have to be careful near water Mum says lakes can be a death trap...rivers too. Even the seaside if you're not careful. Mum says anywhere around water can he unsafe," he added looking a tad gloomy. "You really want to be careful around open water," he said now looking anxious. "You could drown Granny..."

"Yes," she said reflectively," I suppose I could..."

Then she turned to him and seemed to rally.

"Well then young man I expect you're hungry eh?"

He'd rather fancied Fish Fingers, but Granny said she didn't trust the stove.

"It could blow up," she said throwing the small electric cooker a wary glance." It smells funny too, gets too hot I think. No I'll make you a nice sandwich Charlie, boiled ham OK?"

It wasn't as bad as he'd thought it would be, except they were a little dry as she hadn't buttered the bread. He'd peeked in the fridge when she'd sent him off to get a yoghurt for afters thinking she must have run out of butter and was surprised to find three unopened packs there.

When he returned he noted Granny hadn't got a sandwich, but was sipping something from her Best Granny in the World cup that he'd given her the pervious Christmas.

"What have you got Granny?"

"Tinned soup...red," she said with relish, "very tasty... those round thingies ...tomatoes," she said smiling of course, "tomato soup."

"But aren't you supposed to heat that up on the stove?" He asked.

"You can do," she agreed, "but it's just as nice cold...probably better for you," she added grinning at him.

The afternoon progressed with the conversation liberally scattered with 'what's its, thingamy jigs and you know...that thing,' until poor Charlie was exhausted from making educated guessed and weathering the force of Granny's frustration when yet another word escaped her.

Finally it was time for him to take his leave.

"Have a nice cold drink before you go," Granny urged, desperately trying to prolong the visit.

He looked interested so they both mooched over to the fridge to see what was on offer.

He pulled a half bottle of gin out and held it aloft, "What's this Granny?"

"It's gin dear, mother's ruin," she said with a little chuckle. "Although not your mother of course, she's far too sensible. Strong drink is full of all sorts of hidden danger no doubt."

When Charlie just looked mystified she put it back in the fridge.

Well Gloria had finally convinced her to give the bottle a try and occasionally she would imbibe...but it usually just sent her to sleep, so money down the drain she'd concluded.

"What about this?" She said brightly, pulling out a can of strong continental lager. She'd bought it on the off chance that Mister Williams might visit again. But seeing how she'd been there over a year now and no sign of anyone from the Day Centre calling once more, it seemed highly unlikely now.

She held the can up high and sang in her cracking old voice, "A [6]Double Diamond works wonders, works wonders...so drink one today!"

"Granny what are you on about?"

"Oh that was an advert on TV Years ago, my Cyril, Granddad used to like a drink of that."

"But this isn't that what-ever Diamond thingy, it's Carlsberg Granny! Dad drinks this...sometimes." When Mum was out, he thought smiling to himself.

"Well then if it's good enough for Dad I imagine its good enough for you then Sunshine."

"Heck Granny I'm not allowed", he said in awe.

"Oh goodness, you're practically grown up aren't you? A small glass of beer won't hurt," she said snapping the ring pull and pouring out a generous measure.

Charlie thought of those jeering big boys he'd seen in the park just that morning. Calling him a wimp because he wouldn't try the Fiery Jack cider they were passing round. The bottle partly hidden by a plastic bag as they lounged around the war memorial. They were from his new school he knew and only a year or so older than him. Maybe he should get ahead of the game and try alcohol now he thought recklessly...after all it couldn't hurt him.

"I'm telling you he was drunk," Amy shouted her voice almost shrieking now, "anything could have happened to him."

"Look keep it down old girl," said Brian looking anxiously out of the open window where Morris, their neighbour, was washing his car on the next door drive.

"Oh it's too late to worry about the neighbours," she cried following his glance." He was sick at the bus stop and then again in the garden...I don't think many folk missed it."

"Food poisoning," Brian said as if producing a rabbit from a hat. "Maybe it's food poisoning; you know how Ma never reads the sell bys."

"Food poisoning my foot. He admitted it! She gave him some of that awful Carlsberg Special you're so fond of."

"The hell she did," Brian muttered in awe. "Well the boy certainly doesn't do things by halves."

"There's no need to look so damn proud," Amy spat. "This is serious or do you want your doolally mother to turn our boy into an alcoholic?"

"Oh come on Amy love, I don't think it's going to come to that," he said giving her a weak grin.

"Too right it's not," she agreed," because Charlie won't be visiting again."

"Well that's hardly fair the poor dear can't get many visitors."

"Exactly," Amy said with her snake like smile, "that's why you're going at the week-end to check on her. Things must have got worse Brian and it's your responsibility to sort her out...get her the help she needs."

Chapter 9

"I'm sorry Mister Richardson, but your mother isn't the easiest of people to keep tabs on. She is in our Independent Living sector you know. She is able to come and go as she pleases. That was agreed in conjunction with your GP. After all she was only in the early stages of Alzheimer's when she joined us. So how have you found her of late?"

Brian looked sheepish, trying to remember the last time he'd visited his mother. Oh he popped in occasionally on a Saturday, when he was on his way home from golf, the flats being conveniently situated near to the golf club. But it had been a flying visit, just time for a quick cuppa and Ma had seemed pretty much the same as usual. OK maybe she'd let herself go a bit. But as she said what was the point of paying the fancy prices of the in house hair salon if she was just going to sit in her room, with nobody to see it.

"Well why don't you mix a bit more Mum. Go down for lunch in the restaurant, or join the craft club, or maybe go to one of those tea dances?"

"Oh our Brian, what do I want with that? I was done with dancing after your Dad died. Eh, but he was a good dancer was Cyril..."

"Well you need to get out more, chat to the other folk, they seem very pleasant."

She'd pulled a face at that and shuddered, "Not my type Brian, far too posh, full of airs and graces. No I'll keep myself to myself thank you very much."

Then the Matron broke into his thoughts, "She really doesn't mix at all you see Mister Richardson, won't even answer the door when we make the odd spot check. I really think she will be rather difficult when the time comes for our Extra Care Package."

"Um, well maybe it won't come to that just yet," said Brian smiling weakly at her. Good grief he certainly hoped not, the financial implications were considerable. Of course his mother was paying at present, but how long would Dad's money last? he asked himself.

Maybe that was why he turned a blind eye to his mother's obvious decline.

"You really shouldn't have given our Charlie that beer Mum," he said sometime later after she had finally answered his loud knocking.

"What I never!" She said looking askance," Why I haven't seen our Charlie in...um...ages."

"Mum you saw him just a week ago."

"I did?" She asked looking vague.

He sighed deeply, "So how are you keeping?"

It was the night time strolls that finally put the kibosh on her.

What did they call it now, this new place? The other had been Independent living that's it she remembered. Stupid damn name for living a normal life she thought. Now this ruddy place 'Assisted Living', well that wasn't normal that was for sure, more like a glorified prison hospital she thought bitterly.

To be honest, she hadn't been right since she left her home, her real home that is. Number 45 where she'd lived all those years with dear Cyril. They'd brought up their Brian and Patricia there too and it held such happy memories. Memories clearer than what happened yesterday she thought with chagrin.

Patricia she thought, so when did she last cast eyes on her daughter, she really couldn't remember.

Anyway she had more important fish to fry right then.

She looked around the Spartan room. The only thing making it look vaguely homelike the many family photos scattered around the windowsill and filling the fitted wall unit. How had her life shrunk down to this she wondered?

She looked at the clean white walls and narrow bed, from her perch on the ugly, hard bedside chair, made for ease of sitting down and getting up rather than comfort. Oh how she longed for the huge old squashy sofa at number 45 with its tendency to shed its horsehair stuffing. Or she would even prefer the neat little two seater sofa that she'd bought when she moved into the Golden Years Independent Living flat. But here in the Golden Years Annexe For Assisted Living well the only way one could get a comfortable seat was to ask to be taken down to the communal lounge.

Nancy sighed deeply, how long had she been enduring this living hell she wondered? Oh if only she could put the clock back and had curbed her desire to wonder about the streets in the dead of night. Now why on earth did she do that?

It was this damn disease of course. In moments of lucidity she knew that.

It had all started with a feeling of unease as night fell. Then it got worse and worse and she felt positively anxious in the little flat and had to get out and walk, sometimes for most of the night. In some sort of topsy turvy world she now regarded the dark hours as the time she should be up and doing and the daytime for sleeping. Occasionally she would question her rationale; 'you're turning into a darned vampire Nancy my girl,' she had chuckled to herself. Then at other times it seemed perfectly normal to sleep away the day and then go off on her little walks during the night.

It was the second time that she had been brought home in a squad car, after wandering the streets at three in the morning in her nightie and slippers, that some action was taken.

The first time she'd managed to give a plausible explanation, telling the nice young officer that she'd locked herself out and just needed a lift back home, now she had a spare key from a neighbour. The policeman was overdue for his mid shift break, so was happy to oblige and once she seemed settled in he left her with a cheeky grin and a," Take care Ma'am."

Ma'am... she'd rather liked that...of course it should have been Mam...to rhyme with ham if addressing the Queen. The American sounding Mam was rather pleasing and took her back to the westerns of her youth. She's always had a soft spot for those old western heroes. Yes you couldn't beat a good cowboy story she had thought.

The second time did not end so well.

It was a bitter winter's night when a squad car had again pulled up beside her as she marched along in her belted dressing gown and slippers. She hadn't noticed the cold. In fact she'd taken off her slippers and had a little paddle in the duck pond at the edge of the lane. Something about the squelch of the mud between her toes, like the sand of long forgotten beaches. It reminded her of childhood holidays in Rhyl and Blackpool.

They'd been very kind, the girls, for that is what they seemed to Nancy. One blond and buxom had insisted she get in the police car and then had tenderly removed her slippers and dried her feet before wrapping a warm blanket around her shoulders.

The other dark and serious looking said, "So my dear what are you doing out and about at this time of night, won't they be missing you at home?"

Nancy thought back to her little flat and thought that maybe the gin swilling Gloria next door might miss her...given a week or two...but otherwise no.

She shook her head, "No I live alone."

"Oh... so where would that be then dear? And what's your name?" The blond woman asked.

"Nancy," she replied and then had to think hard...it was some flower or other...to do with bees maybe?

Honeycomb... Honeymoon? Oh come on Nancy think...she urged herself....Honeysuckle that was it. "Flat 3 Honeysuckle Corridor," she replied with relief.

"Righto my dearie, so where is the corridor then? Is it in one of the Homes?"

Nancy looked thoughtful, "I think so."

"The Eventide Rest Home maybe?"

Nancy shook her head.

"Vale View.... The Lamp House.... Mycote Gardens?"

Nancy was getting more and more confused, but then the dark one noticed she was clutching her oversized handbag.

"Should we take a little peek in the bag Madam, see if there are any clues?"

Nancy reluctantly relinquished her hold on the bag and the contents were studied carefully by the two police officers.

A jar of Marmite...unopened. Some peppermints, a small calendar dated five years previously, a purse containing family photos and £3.75 and finally right at the bottom a small address book with a doe eyed weeping puppy on the front.

The blond one, Doris, Nancy noted the other one called her...took a peek. Funny how these old fashioned names came back into vogue Nancy thought, she had a school friend called Doris, red hair...temper to match.

The sharp eyed Doris had noticed' this book belongs to: Nancy Richardson, 'scrawled on the front page.

"Nancy Richardson is it?" She asked now.

Nancy nodded.

"Good so let's see if your address is in here shall we?"

However after careful perusal there was still no Care Home address listed.

"How about this," asked Doris," a Brian Richardson, is he a relative?"

Nancy looked thoughtful, and then her face cleared," Why yes that's our Brian...my little boy."

"So shall we go and pay a visit then dear, see if he knows where you live? Maybe get him to look after you tonight. I think you could use a bath to warm those tootsies up couldn't you," the blond Doris quipped.

So that had been it.

Brian was not pleased to have the police hammering on the door at 4 AM and Amy even less so.

"For goodness sake show them in Brian before they wake up all the neighbours," Amy had said peering anxiously around the close.

She'd stayed the night at their Brian's place, with only young Charlie pleased to see her the following morning as they sat around the breakfast table.

"I just can't fathom what you were doing wandering around the streets in the middle of the night Mother," said Brian, pausing as he buttered his toast to peer at his mother.

"Maybe she was going on an adventure," Charlie piped up, "like the Burglar Granny in my story book. "

Amy sighed, "If you've finished your cereal go and get your homework book Charlie the bus will be here any minute."

"Laters Granny," he said cheerfully hugging her before he ran off to do as he was told.

Meanwhile Amy threw Brian a meaningful look and tipped her head towards the kitchen door.

"I'll make some more toast Mum," she said getting up and hurrying out.

After a moment Brian said," Uh...um yes, I'll help you dear."

Once ensconced in the kitchen Amy whispered, "What are we going to do with her?"

Brian shrugged, "Dunno, I suppose I'd better drop her off back at the flat on my way to work. It means I'll be a tad late, but can't be helped I suppose."

"No you idiot... I mean about this she hissed. What that PC said about her paddling in the duck pond...wandering about wearing next to nothing she could have drowned or at least caught her death, it can't go on Brian. It will have to be dealt with."

"Dealt with?" He asked blankly.

"Well you'll have to call Social Services explain, because as sure as eggs are eggs, they'll be on to you if you don't.

"Huh, why should they do that?"

"Because the police will have reported back to the Social of course. Hand in fist with the Social Services they are. I'd get in quick if I were you, before they come around charging us with neglect or some such thing. "

Chapter 10

As it happened the Social Services were on the ball and indeed they did contact Brian, albeit with some sound advice and help rather than the chastisement he was expecting. That's when it had been decided that she was ready, indeed more than ready, to move to the Golden Years Extra Care package and move into the Assisted Living annexe.

All that had been several weeks ago and now Nancy sat in the hard upright chair, strategically placed by the window and looked out at the cold landscape stretching out beyond. Yes it had been the night time wandering that had done for her she remembered now. That night when she'd met those nice police girls Doris...and uh... well the other one.

Of course it hadn't been their fault she'd been thrown in jail...and had no chance of throwing a 6 and ever getting out again, she thought with a sad smile.

 It had been down to that Amy, she always had been spiteful. Ever since the wedding when she'd overheard Nancy talking to her best friend, she hadn't really meant it anyway...it was the drink talking. She'd had three Sherries on an empty stomach, which was a recipe for disaster in anybody's book she thought now. When she'd called

Amy manipulative and a money grabber, what she'd really meant was that she was clever and ambitious, it had just come out all wrong. Then of course there were tears and recriminations with Amy declaring that Nancy had spoiled her big day. But in reality it was because Amy couldn't join in and enjoy a drink, what with her being three months pregnant and all. But of course that was never discussed.

So now Amy had the last laugh, Nancy thought once more surveying the Spartan room and less than inspiring view beyond the window.

There was a knock at the door, just as she was nodding off as usual and there was Beatrice. The cheerful West Indian lady had come to check on her and exchange a bit of banter, so she called the odd piece of news or gossip.

Truth be told Beatrice was the best of the bunch... Monday Wednesday and Friday were her days and alternate Saturdays.

"But not Sunday Nancy my lovely because that is the Lord's Day and has to be kept special don't you think?" She'd said.

Nancy did indeed...Never a Sunday had passed without a Sunday joint, come hail, rain or [8]Mrs

Thatcher. Cyril always had money for the essentials of life he used to say and what was life without a good slice of roast beef and a Yorkshire pudding of a Sunday lunchtime?

They weren't big Church goers. Just the usual, Christenings, Weddings and Funerals and of course the Midnight Service on Christmas Eve...they never missed that. It wasn't that she was a complete heathen she told folks...if they asked. Dearie me no, she'd been no stranger to the inside of a Church growing up. Morning Service, Sunday school, Evensong, she'd attended them all in her time. In fact she'd met her dear Cyril at the Church Youth Club.

But then after they were married and the children came along, there never seemed to be the time. After Cyril retired they'd been asked to attend. The Vicar had called, said he wasn't about to do a hard sell, chuckling at his own joke. But he'd love to see them next Sunday. Well they'd tried it. But it really wasn't their cup of tea. All that intoning and incense, it got on Cyril's chest so they didn't go again.

Maybe she'd prefer Beatrice's Church she mused now. All that Gospel singing and clapping sounded quite jolly.

Now Beatrice beamed at her, "We've a surprise for you all down in the lounge," she said her eyes twinkling with delight.

"Eh not that wretched housey-housey man again," Nancy said with disgust. "I can't stand him. Too damn fond of himself, way he prances around calling us all his special ladies."

"What dear? The housey-housey man?" Beatrice asked raising a questioning eyebrow.

"You know... damn it. What's the dratted word?" Nancy asked angrily. "Numbers...calling out... silly comments two fat ladies...you know!"

"Oh," said Beatrice the light of understanding dawning, "you mean the Bingo caller Mr Evans, of course and you call House when you've won, isn't that right?"

Nancy nodded slightly mollified now the word had at last been found, Bingo of course, she knew that.

Then she sighed deeply. It was happening all the time now. Hardly an hour went by when she couldn't recall some simple everyday word. It used to be the difficult ones, like Robinson's Marmalade. Funny she could remember the Robinson's but not the marmalade word. They'd had fun and games with that one. Orange sticky stuff...in a jar...on toast. Unfortunately it had been Una the Polish lady volunteer on duty that morning and she's been totally foxed...her English not being too good as yet.

"Marmalade," she said now, looking off to the middle distance, "It's marmalade of course."

"What dear?"

Nancy sighed, "Nothing...so what's this big surprise then? It better be worth it."

"Oh it will be," Beatrice reassured her. "So what's it to be a nice little walk or use the chair?"

Nancy hated the wheelchair with a vengeance, talk about 'old git' she said to herself every time she sat in the darned thing. But on the other hand, her legs had begun to feel decidedly wonky of late. There had been that dreadful time just a couple of weeks ago when she'd made it down to the residents' lounge in the lift. But then when it came to walking back, well her legs just wouldn't cooperate. She'd been forced to call for one of the staff to go and fetch her chair and that in front of that nice Mr Shannon too. Oh the embarrassment of it all.

Once she was seated in the wheelchair Beatrice took her down to the lounge where their seemed to be hi jinks going on Nancy noted, from the lively chatter coming from the large sunny room. Beatrice parked her up next to Mr Day. He was peering into space in his usual zombie like manner and Nancy mentally rolled her eyes. Mr Day was one of the less responsive residents and she secretly thought he should be in the hospice. He was as thin as a wraith and neither talked or indeed responded at all. She hated to look at him, truth be known, as he was the embodiment of what would eventually befall them all. Or so she thought, and who wanted to be reminded of that on a daily bases. She averted her gaze and then looked around the room.

It took a few seconds for her to see exactly what was going on and then she thought she must be having one of her funny turns, because there just a few yards away from her stood a small Shetland pony.

She did a double take and then looked up to Beatrice for reassurance.

"It's alright honey you ain't seeing things," she said cheerfully. "This little chap is called Sonny and he's one of those therapy horses."

The residents were all seated in a large circle and Sonny made his way patiently around them, stopping to be petted and crooned over.

As he came closer Nancy began to smile, he was a pretty little chap she thought. Now what was that colouring...a blond mane and beige coat? Uh...Palomino that's right. She remembered it from Patricia's horse book. She grimaced...can't remember marmalade but you know a Palomino when you see one she said to herself. Bonkers girl you're pure bonkers.

Then she thought back to her daughter Patricia. Eh the lass had been so keen to go horse riding. But of course it wasn't within their reach. Maybe ten minutes on a donkey on Blackpool front, but that was it. She wondered what had become of her daughter, when had she seen her last? She couldn't remember. Well no change there then she thought ruefully.

But by then Sonny had reached her and the young owner was encouraging her to stroke the velvety muzzle.

She looked into his large eyes with their impossibly long lashes and fell in love. He blew gently through his nostrils and bowed his head, his eyes closing in seeming ecstasy as she gently scratched behind his ears. There was a slight odour of warm horse about him and she was immediately transported back to her seven year old self petting the milkman's horse...strangely named Roger. She had loved Roger with a passion and had cried for a week when he was replaced by a small electric van.

Now she looked up at the young owner and said with a chuckle, "So is he house trained then dear? "

The girl nodded," Oh yes absolutely."

Nancy shook her head enjoying the joke and then cast a glance down at the highly polished parquet flooring. The little chap seemed to be wearing sort of canvas shoes, to preserve the floor...but certainly not a nappy.

"He can count too," the girl continued, "tell him a number under ten."

She did as requested and right away the little pony tapped out five with his dainty hoof...much to the surprised admiration of all.

Then just moments later Sonny nudged his owner several times with his head.

"There you see," the lass said," he's asking to go out," and she quickly took him out through the open French windows to relieve him-self on the lawn.

"Well I'll be," muttered Nancy, "whatever next."

However if the amassed company had thought being housetrained and counting were the height of Sonny's repartee they were sorely mistaken. Because his next trick way surpassed anything else he had achieved. He got a reaction from Mr Day!

The gaunt elderly gentleman had been just staring into the middle distance when Sonny joined him. The horse seemed to instinctively know what was required of him and he came close to the old man...his head practically in his lap and then blew gently through his nostrils. Whether it was the faint odour of horse or the soft whinny that evoked the response nobody knew. But just seconds later Mr Day focused on Sonny...he gave a broad grin and gently started to stroke him, his tired old eyes full of joy.

Chapter 11

All this had been a couple of months ago and Nancy hadn't been out of her room since. She was disinclined to socialise with the other 'inmates ', as she thought of the other residents. All but the pleasant Mr Shannon that is, they had got on well. He'd lived in the next street to Nancy and Cyril and they had a few friends in common. But then just the day after Sonny's visit he'd upped and died.

"It was his heart," Beatrice had told her, "he could have gone at anytime, but the end was swift and now he's at peace," she added smiling gently at Nancy.

"You're sure of that are you?" Nancy asked, her grief making her sound angry and churlish.

"It's all any of us can hope for my lovely," Beatrice said softly before going off to make Nancy a nice cup of tea, the cure all at the Golden Years Assisted Living annexe.

Now a few months later Nancy sat in her chair pulled up to the large picture window and peered out at the distant washing blowing on a line, her view the rear of a modern housing estate.

It must be Monday she thought to herself, "Monday is washday," she said out loud.

She cast her mind back to when Brian and Patricia were babies. A full line of snowy white nappies on the line before nine was always her goal. None of those dreadful plastic disposable things filling up landfill sites...no not in her day.

She thought back to her neighbours Rita to the left hand side. Crikey she'd been a stuck up bitch when she first arrived at the terrace, all fur coat and no knickers, that's what her old ma would have said.

Married to a shirt salesman and thought she was the
[9]bee's knees just because they ran an Austin 7.
Always off for a little spin in the Cheshire
countryside of a Sunday. Well she soon had that
knocked out of her when Graham took up with a
shop assistant from [10]Lewis's and left, taking the
Austin 7 with him. Well after that Nancy and Betty,
on the other side, rallied around, helped the poor
cow out. Always on hand with a bit of left over
stew...or a loaf to see her through to the end of the
week.

But there was a healthy rivalry between the three
neighbours and it was always a race to see who
would have their whites on the line first on a
Monday morning and to [11]donkey stone the front
step too.

What had become of Rita and Betty she wondered
now? Young Pete lived in Betty's old house and she,
Barry and the kids had moved out to the Wirral in
about 1970. As to Rita she had remarried and gone
abroad. Canada that's right she'd married that nice
Canadian boy. Took the kids and even the dog and
moved off to Vancouver, or some such place. Funny
she could remember all that and not what was for
lunch yesterday she reflected.

Well there it was she was stuck with just the lovely Beatrice now as friend and confidant. Because let's face it love you're not going to get any sense out of the rest of those poor buggers downstairs she said to herself, referring to the other patients.

Yes her boy Brian visited only once every [12] Preston Guild, along with her little ray of sunshine Charlie. As to that stuck up wife of his, well it had been last Christmas when she'd last clapped eyes on her. Then it was just a 'fleeting visit', "so much to do, you understand don't you Mum."

Oh she understood alright and what wouldn't she have given to be in that whirlwind of preparations for a family Christmas. Rushing around the shops for the last minute presents for Brian and Patricia's stockings. Woolworths had been the best bet for those little gifts. Tubs of Bubble Stuff and a handful of Pick N Mix in a little white paper bag...Always down in the toe of the stocking, a Cracker at the top.

Then on Christmas Eve finally the turkey stuffed and dressed and happily roasting away in the slow oven overnight, they'd listen to Christmas carols on the wireless. The smell of Cyril's cigar, the yearly present from his boss, permeated the little house. How she had loved that smell, it really was the smell of Christmas... dear Cyril and his cigar.

Nowadays what did she have to look forward to? A tasteless mashed up meal of white meat, allegedly turkey, but who knew? It certainly didn't seem to have any breast or leg merely squares of greyish meat smothered in salty gravy with a mixture of mashed potato and the odd sprout on the side, washed down with a glass of some disgusting tasting wine. What was wrong with a little bottle of Babycham...after all it was Christmas! Then there would be tepid plum pudding, swiftly followed by the Queen's Speech. No the King's speech now she suddenly remembered, young Charles was the boss man now...and dear Queen Elizabeth 11 gone to a better place.

Some lucky folk had visitors, but the residents mostly fell asleep in front of the TV before they were roused early for a sandwich. Then the bedtime ritual was followed an hour early, so the staff could get home and enjoy what was left of the day.

She was dragged from her reverie by Beatrice bustling in looking excited and waving an envelope aloft.

"You have a letter!" She said her honest, kindly face wreathed in smiles, "I do believe it's from your best friend in Australia!"

"Susan...Susan's written?" Nancy asked in excitement. "You know I was just thinking about Christmas too!"

Beatrice frowned slightly and then said, "Well you don't want to be thinking of that just yet my lovely, it's only September."

Nancy looked surprised, but recovered quickly.

"Well she's certainly ahead of the game with her Christmas letter," she said cheerfully squinting at the envelope now being proffered to her. Funny the writing looked different, but then with her eyesight nothing looked normal anymore she thought with a sigh.

"Go on Beatrice dear, open it up and read it to me do, "she said with the impatience of a child.

Beatrice sank onto the bed and ripping open the letter, being careful to save the stamp for Charlie, she started to read.

Dear Mrs Richardson, It is with great sorrow that I must inform you of the death of my beloved mother Susan.

At this Nancy gasped a hand shooting to her mouth...her eyes wide with shock.

"Oh dearie me I am so sorry," Beatrice said reaching out a comforting hand.

Nancy swallowed hard and said, "Go on... "

Beatrice looked back to the sheet of notepaper held in her now trembling hand...took a deep breath and continued.

I know you and Mum were best friends all your lives and she spoke of you often. After Dad died it was her dearest wish to return to the UK, but sadly it wasn't to be and she passed away from cancer just last month. She is I believe now at peace and hopefully in a better place, the letter concluded.

I send you all good wishes from Melbourne, James White (son).

"Little Jamie," Nancy whispered," kind of him to think of me...he was a good boy... A sweet baby," she added and she closed her eyes.

"Are you all right my lovely? Would you like a nice cup of tea?" Beatrice asked.

"No thanks I'd like to be alone," Nancy said not opening her eyes.

She waited until she heard the door close quietly and then let the tears flow.

After a while she had to speak sharply to herself, "Eh Nancy lass stop being such a cry baby!" She said firmly and dug about under her pillow for her hankie. She wiped her eyes and blew her nose loudly before relaxing back and remembering.

She had met Susan on the first day of school, the Mixed Infants Department of the local council school. They'd shared a desk from day one and had spent most of the first morning howling in unison at being abandoned by their mothers into this hellish place called school. However by the afternoon they were beginning to accept their lot and by home time they were firm friends.

That friendship was to last throughout their childhood and teens. They had chickenpox together and enjoyed birthday parties and the long summer holidays in each other's company. Later they shared the misery of their first broken hearts once they started dating boys. Then when the frog kissing was over and they were betrothed they were each bridesmaid to the other. Nancy marrying Cyril, who she had known from Sunday school and Susan Brad, who she met in the war. He was with the Australian

Air Corp based nearby and it had been love at first sight.

Then the children came along... Brian first and then Susan gave birth to James.

"What a sweet child," Nancy said again softly to herself. James and Brian were firm friends and then Susan gave birth to young Archie the same year as she had Patricia.

Oh she'd known there was something wrong right away. His eyes were sort of oriental, she remembered and it wasn't long before Susan's tearful admission that he was a Mongol. Uh what did they call them now? Down's syndrome that was it. She paused and mentally patted herself on the back for that one. She remembered now. Brian had pulled her up about it once, not too long ago. Said it wasn't politically correct or some such thing...it was called Down's now. Well the poor little mite hadn't lived long anyway. That was when Brad said he wanted to go home, move the family back to Melbourne where he'd been born... a fresh start for them all he'd said.

Eh but she'd missed Susan. It was like a light had gone out of her life, nobody, but nobody knew her as well as Susan. Oh they'd kept in touch alright, writing three or four times a year with all the news but it wasn't the same. Then what...about a dozen years ago now she'd visited. What a time they'd had together. At first Nancy had hardly recognised this buxom woman with the greying hair and Aussie accent. But then once they got chatting she was still the same old Susan underneath. What fun it had been revisiting old haunts, reminiscing....and oh how she had cried when she left.

Now she sniffed again. What would she do without dear Susan...her last friend gone?

Chapter 12

"I just thought you should know," Matron said, her voice down the phone sounding slightly judgemental.

"As I say Mr Richardson, the shock of losing her best friend seems to have accelerated the illness to some extent. She is getting more and more difficult to communicate with I'm sorry to say. I really feel that a visit might help her. Bring her out of herself if you know what I mean?"

Brian muttered on about pressure of work and family commitments for a few embarrassing minutes before agreeing to visit at his earliest possible convenience as requested by Matron.

"Yes, yes Matron, Saturday then...yes... goodbye."

"What... take Charlie with you? I don't think so... do you?" Amy said sarcastically. "It could scar the boy for life if she really has gone completely potty now."

"You're all heart aren't you," Brian shot back.

 Then wheedling said, "Well will you come then my little princess, um...please?"

Amy rolled her eyes, "How many times have I told you not to call me that...it's so common. And no I won't it's my baking day on Saturday, you know that!"

"Couldn't you do it Sunday, after all there may not be that much time left if what that old Dragon was saying is true. Seems Mum has stopped eating and won't talk much either."

"It won't be too taxing for you then will it, not having to make conversation," she said turning away," and there'll be a nice hot apple pie waiting when you come home," she added before heading off to the kitchen.

Late Saturday morning, after his junior league match, Charlie did what he'd been doing once a month or so since Granny had taken to her bed. He visited the home on his way back from the footy.

He hadn't mentioned it at home as Ma tended to fuss and at fourteen now he reckoned he could do what he wanted in his free time, within reason that was. He wasn't part of the set that whiled away Saturday afternoon in the park drinking cheap cider. His little brush with Granny's Carlsberg Special had quashed any desire to try alcohol again anytime soon. Nope he usually caught up with his best mate Vinny and they would spend the afternoon round at his house, playing computer games, eating crisps and discussing girls.

Now however he was on a mission to visit his Gran, making sure he bypassed that miserable Matron woman who had once told him he was too young to visit patients alone. He tried to explain that it wasn't a patient, but his Gran. However Matron would have none of it and merely said,' run along sonny, I'll tell granny you called.'

So now he had an arrangement with Beatrice who waited for him when she went on shift on the last Saturday of the month and let him in via the staff entrance.

Now as he tapped on the door and entered he stood back looking shocked, Granny seemed to have really changed since last time and her tiny form hardly registered beneath the colourful duvet. She looked awful he thought privately.

"Granny hasn't been eating too much," Beatrice said softly," and she's not got too much to say for herself right now either Charlie boy. But let's hope you bring her out of herself a little um?"

Charlie nodded and steeled himself to go and take a seat by the bed. After a few minutes Nancy opened her eyes and looking around the room her gaze finally came to rest on Charlie and then up to where Beatrice was beaming at her.

"Look whose come to see you Nancy," she said.

Nancy had been having a lovely dream about that time they'd taken Brian and Pat to the seaside at Morecombe and now here was young Brian come to visit.

"Eh, our Brian, you've come to see your old Mam," she said smiling for the first time in weeks.

"But Granny I've told you before I'm..."

Then he felt Beatrice's hand on his shoulder, "Just go with the flow Charlie," she said softly, "maybe Granny will remember who you are later, but now it's just good she's talking again, you understand honey?"

Charlie nodded, after all it wasn't the first time she'd mistaken him for Dad and he could cope with that.

They had a good chat about a holiday they'd had in someplace called Morecombe that Charlie had never heard of. Then Beatrice brought a nice cup of tea for Granny and a coke for him. Granny drank the tea at least but refused an arrowroot biscuit, although

Charlie knew they were her favourites...after Hobnobs of course.

Then they chatted about school and Charlie's football team for a while, with the youngster doing most of the talking, but Granny taking a lively interest. Then it was finally time for him to go and she shed a tear as per usual, but brightened up when he said he'd be back soon.

She was lying there going over the visit in her head, goodness young Brian really was growing up fast she thought. I must get out of this damn place and get home soon she pledged. Maybe he'd bring his little sister next time... Pat.

Just as Charlie was sneaking out of the back door of the Care Home, dodging Matron, his father was parking at the front.

There was a knock on Nancy's door and that officious Matron stood there beaming at her like she was really pleased to see her, two faced hag Nancy thought belligerently.

"Look who has come to see you Nancy dear, it's your son Brian," she said cheerfully.

Nancy stared icily at the balding middle aged man with the slight paunch and then back at Matron, and merely shook her head stubbornly, and cried." Not my Brian."

"Of course it is dear, don't be silly," Matron said, losing her smile and backing off. "It's just been a while... I'll leave you to get reacquainted."

"Beatrice!" Nancy called out desperately, not wanting to be left alone with this imposter.

"She's busy my dear," Matron called over her shoulder, closing the door quickly behind her.

Beatrice, was currently holding the hand of Ethel Myers, down the corridor, who was about to shuffle off this mortal coil. No, Beatrice wouldn't be back with Nancy for some time Matron knew... But in the meantime she was in the safe hands of her son.

Nancy peered at the stranger with frightened eyes.

"Mum... Mum it's me Brian," Brian said anxiously.

She just shook her head and continued to stare at him. Goodness Brian had only just left, who was this aging man with the glasses and intense expression?

The more Brian tried to explain who he was the more upset Nancy became.

He must be one of her old flames she finally decided. One of the ones she'd stepped out with before agreeing to marry dear Cyril...that was it. Come to think of it he favoured Cyril somewhat, around the eyes... the set of the chin. That's what must have attracted her to him she decided. But it had always been Cyril...from day one when they met in the Sunday school and then later really got together at the youth club. She closed her eyes and tried to remember.

Brian sat there for a long time watching her as she drifted off to sleep.

"Mum...mummy," he whispered...but it was no good, she had gone from him.

He finally arose and kissing her tenderly on the forehead left. He stopped at the door and looked back once more...before sadly turning and walking away.

Chapter 13

That was to be the beginning of the end for Nancy had she happened to think about it, but she did not.

She had begun to stop focusing on the here and now and went off to what she called the 'Then Time'...the past. The time when life was as she wanted it to be. Oh she was heartily sick of the constant frustrations of daily life. She was sick of the mental fog that seemed to be surrounding her more and more frequently and her physical limitations.

Now she was bed bound she had to put up with all the indignities that entailed. When she was being washed, dressed, or toileted, that's when she had started drifting off into the 'Then Time.'

At first it had been voluntary but now more and more often she was dwelling in that strange dream like world. It was a place where the past was more convincing and real than the present and where she could relax and really be herself once more.

Occasionally a face would loom before her to try and drag her back to the 'Here and Now'. That pretty black girl...she was vaguely familiar... Bea...bee something was it? She sighed at the effort and closed her eyes.

"Come on my lovely a nice cup of tea here for you," Beatrice pleaded.

She'd drunk the tea, anything for a quiet life she thought as she lay back against the pillows. It was hard to swallow now though and she hated that feeling of choking. She watched as the pretty dark girl made her comfortable once more and turned for the door with a cheery, "See you later love..."

It was just as the door was about to close that he put his nose around and peered in at her...then wagging his tail he dashed into the room, just before the door closed, and leapt onto her bed. His whole body was quivering with delight as he squirmed into her arms licking her face and whimpering in joy.

"Scamper...Scamp, what on earth are you doing here?" She asked patting him and revelling in his warm muscular body now curling up beside her.

 Scamper, the Border Collie cross had been the heart of their family when the children were growing up and they had all been devastated when he'd finally died of old age. He'd been what fourteen... no fifteen when he'd been put down. Yet here he was back again and looking much like that cheeky little puppy they'd fallen in love with all those years ago. Nancy didn't question it as this was par for the course these days and she just accepted it happily.

"Eh but I've missed you Scamper lad," she crooned to him and the little dog yawned and settled down to sleep beside her.

The following morning when she awoke he was still there looking up into her face, his tail beating a tattoo on the duvet.

She stroked him absently and looked out of the window to see a winter wonderland beyond.

Then her attention was taken as a young girl entered without knocking and stood grinning down at her and smiling.

"Morning Nancy love, cold enough for you is it?" She asked nodding to the icy scene beyond the picture window, although it was actually suffocatingly hot in the bedroom as per usual, Nancy thought fleetingly.

"Looks like we're in for a white Christmas," the ginger haired girl continued as she expertly shook out the duvet, not expecting an answer.

Nancy briefly acknowledged that Christmas must be finally on the way and then she drifted off taking Scamp with her for a nice long walk. The usual one, down the street, first left at the bottom and into the municipal park where he had a good run around, lifted his leg over the ornamental rose bush and the War Memorial before running off to play with one of the other local dogs. She sat on a bench and watched him fondly.

Oh but it was chilly...hadn't someone said that earlier? No matter, but her hands and feet were freezing. She'd call him in a minute and get off home for a nice hot cuppa...and some Pedigree Chum for Scamp. Give him ideas above his station she thought chuckling, there certainly wasn't too much pedigree blood circulating in Scamps veins. But what he lacked in blue blood he made up for in his cheeky character and loving ways she thought happily.

It was as they were on the way home that Cyril joined them.

"Well this is a turn up for the book," she said happily," what are you doing here at this time?"

"Finished work early seeing as it's a Friday and nearly Christmas thought I'd surprise you my lovely.

"Eh, but it's good to see you our Cyril, funny but it seems an age," she said suddenly feeling anxious for some unknown reason.

"What are you on about Nancy heck it was only at breakfast and as I remember you gave me a good lambasting about leaving my fishing tackle in the hallway again."

"Did I?" she said vaguely, "Well like you said nearly Christmas, got to get everything shipshape...before the invasion of the outlaws."

Cyril chuckled at her usual little joke and said, "You love the in-laws, Ma and Pa, as much as I do my girl and well you know it."

"That's as maybe but it doesn't stop your dear Ma running a finger along places looking for dust."

"Well she'll not find it in our place you keep it like a little palace my lovely."

As they neared the gate he said," I'll just have a quick cup of tea with you. Then I'll be off to my shed to give Pat's doll's house a last lick of paint. You be sure to head her off at the pass if she looks like she's heading that way when she comes home from school."

Nancy chuckled, "Head her off at the pass? You and young Brian are addicted to those westerns on the telly, if it's not Bonanza, its Wells Fargo or that Laramie."

"All good clean fun my lovely...and I know Brian's going to just love the six gun I've bought him. It sounds like a real gun with them caps," he added with undisguised delight.

"Just don't let him go frightening our Scamp with it," she said firmly before going off to put the kettle on.

"Nancy...Nancy dear it's time for your tea," Beatrice said her pretty face smiling down at the old woman in the bed.

Nancy stared at her and then looked around for Cyril. What where the heck was she...and where was her kitchen...her husband...and little Scamp?

"Come on Nancy, drink it up," Beatrice said deftly holding the feeding cup to Nancy's lips.

She jerked it away, spilling some on the quilt and cried out in an agony of despair, "Go away I want my Cyril and I want to go home! "

Those were the last words she ever uttered...

As the days moved on towards Christmas Nancy spent her time drifting off and refused to speak or even acknowledge any of her visitors...or the staff, in fact she seemed hardly aware of their presence.

Chapter 14

It was Christmas Eve when the phone call came. Brian had already started the holiday, having finished work a few days earlier. It was one of the perks of management, but he was somewhat regretting his decision as he was caught up in all Amy's last minute preparations.

"Hang it all Amy," he said after breakfast, "it's my kid sister coming to stay not the Queen of Sheba!"

"Um," retorted Amy waspishly, "she may not be the Queen, but she certainly acts like one with all those airs and graces of hers. Not to mention all those designer clothes she'll doubtless be draped in. And here's me in my Mark's and Sparks jumper and skirt."

"For goodness sake Amy we've been through all this before, of course the girl has smart clothes she has to dress well as a business executive, goes with the job. Anyway she's never had kids, and now not even a husband to spend money on since the divorce."

"I don't see why she couldn't have invited us down to London for a few days she's plenty of space in that luxury apartment of hers," Amy replied ignoring his comment.

"You know perfectly well why, she wants to spend some time with Mum, she's hardly clapped eyes on her these last twelve months."

"Well I don't know why she's bothering it's not like the old girl talks anymore. She doesn't know us and won't know Pat either, so what is the point?" Amy asked arms akimbo.

"Well it's too late to change the plans anyway," Brian said peering at his watch, "she'll be well on her way now, in fact should arrive in time for lunch."

"Lunch, did you say?" Amy shrieked," What makes you think I've got time to start preparing lunch, with all I've got to do?"

That was when the phone rang and with a sigh of relief Brian went across the room to answer it, whilst Amy sank down on an armchair and listened to the one way conversation.

"What are you sure? I uh mean this isn't the first time you've thought..."

"Oh...oh yes I see...uh indeed yes."

"As soon as I can, yes...uh thank you...goodbye..."

Brian collapsed down on the chair by the phone looking ashen.

For once Amy was genuinely sympathetic.

"Goodness Brian what's the matter?" she asked getting up and moving over to him.

"It's Mum," he said," that was Matron, she said she's dying."

Amy rolled her eyes, "No she won't be they said that before...she can't anyway its Christmas," she added.

Brian just stared blankly at that and said, "Well its true this time, Christmas or not."

Then getting up said, "I'll tell our Charlie, maybe he'd like to hang out with his mate Bill next door. Sid and Irene will keep an eye on him, give him his lunch and that," he said vaguely.

"Why I'm here aren't I?" Amy replied looking puzzled.

"You'll be at the Home with me," Brian said firmly, in a voice that brooked no argument. "We'll just wait on our Pat arriving and then we'll drive over," he said before leaving the room, to go upstairs and inform Charlie of this latest development.

Amy sighed, no arguing with Brian when he had one of his, what she called stubborn moods on him and she went off to change. She'd wear her new cashmere jumper, that would show Pat that she knew what was what, she thought with a wicked smile.

She met Brian coming back down the stairs and he said," It's no good he doesn't want to go next door, he's coming with us."

"What to a deathbed scene are you mad it will scar the child for life!" Amy said hysterically.

"For God's sake get a grip Amy, the boy is fifteen, old enough to make his own decisions about this kind of thing, he's a young man now not a child."

Amy stopped in her tracks and looked into her husband's weary eyes and felt a sudden stab of guilt, swiftly followed by compassion, remembering suddenly just how dear he really was to her.

"You're right of course Bri...and I'm sorry I'm being such a bitch. I'll just get changed and be down in a jiffy."

000000

Back in the care home a group of neat little primary school children lined up outside the Care Home Lounge, some wriggling with excitement in anticipation of the afternoon's events. However Miss Clarke their teacher quickly brought them to order and with a firm," Robert Jones, lead on," the children marched into the room.

There was a ripple of equally excited chatter from the residents, but they quickly settled as the children were introduced and started singing the first carol, 'Away in a Manger.'

The sweet, pure notes drifted through the open doorway and up the stairs.

Nancy shifted in her sleep, "Eh," she said to herself," the carol singers are coming down the street," and rushing to the door she threw it open, all the better to hear.

As she stood there clutching a plate of mince pies to distribute to the singers, when they finally reached her house, she mentally ticked off all the jobs on her list.

All the presents now arranged around the tree. Cyril had given her a hand with that, the large doll's house and Brian's six gun and Sherriff's badge in prime position. Plus various other little gifts from friends and family. The children were long in bed, their stockings waiting to be filled by Santa. Well when he came back from the pub she thought indulgently.

It had become the tradition that Cyril took his Ma and Pa out to the local for an hour or so on Christmas Eve to give her a bit of peace to gather her thoughts. And how she relished that little bit of peace...an oasis in a rumble tumble happy Christmas. Once the carol singers had accepted her largess with many thanks and moved on she returned to the kitchen where she checked on the Turkey in the slow oven. Then pouring herself a modest glass of sweet sherry, she sat down in her rocker and relaxed back closing her eyes...peace perfect peace.

She was awoken sometime later by the sound of someone weeping softly.

She opened her eyes a crack and could just make out a smartly dressed blond woman wiping her eyes and sniffing loudly.

"Oh heck our Pat will you stop taking on so," another woman said irritably.

"Goodness knows you've had enough time to visit...if you could have pulled yourself way from that darned job of yours."

Nancy switched her glance to the other speaker and saw a thin, sallow faced woman in a pink posh looking jumper that really didn't suit her at all.

Then a sad faced man with grey hair and a paunch, said, "For goodness sake you two have some respect."

Good grief she thought who the hell were these people and what were they doing in her kitchen and then she opened her eyes wider and saw she wasn't in her cosy kitchen at all. Where the heck was she...and she gasped in shock and distress.

"See, see you've upset her," Brian admonished.

"Then taking her hand said, "It's me Mum... Brian."

"What...what on earth was this strange, weary looking man saying? Brian, he wasn't her Brian. She wondered if she was having some sort of dream...or nightmare more like.

Then someone else spoke.

"Granny... Granny it's me Charlie."

At this she turned her head and smiled at the handsome young man. Who was the young boy, she had no idea. But there was something vaguely familiar... she racked her brains, but it was no good....it had gone.

"She knows you Charlie," Brian whispered," She's pleased to see you, you can tell."

However the effort of trying to remember was too much for Nancy and once again she had that feeling that she had forgotten how to breathe. Odd it was. It had been happening more and more often over the last hour or so...and she concentrated on her breathing... in...out....in...out....in....out....

Then she was suddenly aware of that oh so familiar smell of Christmas, Cyril's cigar. The warm woody odour permeating the room and she opened her eyes wide.

Just behind Charlie stood Cyril, puffing away at his cigar and grinning at her.

"Come on lass it's time," he said holding out a hand to her.

She smiled and with a feeling of overwhelming love and happiness she rose out of her body and taking his hand they drifted off up towards the ceiling.

It seemed perfectly normal to be viewing her worn out old body from upon high and the folk around the bed too.

Then it all came to her like a thunderbolt as her memory returned with force. The woman in the smart clothes was her daughter Pat of course and the one in that dreadful pink jumper Brian's Amy! Well the poor mare never did have any taste or colour sense she thought fleetingly. Brian was genuinely upset too. Oh, but when had he begun to look so old and defeated she thought as she studied her son. Then something happened to cheer her. Amy put her arm around Brian and she was comforting him... that was a step in the right direction Nancy conceded.

Then she finally looked down at the gangly youth who was sitting head bowed. Oh her dear Charlie, her Sunshine. He was a good boy, the best of the bunch she said softly to herself. The only one who had accepted everything that sod of an illness had thrown at her. He'd stuck by her through it all bless the lad.

Then she saw Brian put an arm around his son and he said, "She was ready to go Charlie boy... and she knew you at the end didn't she...gave you that big smile just before she went."

Now Nancy turned to the real recipient of her smile.

"It was so awful Cyril, I'd forgotten them all, my family...I feel so bad...how could I have done that?"

Cyril shook his wise old head and said, "Nay lass, everything happens for a reason and maybe one day we'll understand it all. And maybe our Pat and Brian will learn something from it all too, like a little understanding and compassion," he said quietly.

"It wasn't easy for them," Nancy said, "it's hard to see your Mam lose her mind I imagine...to change so much...not even know them anymore."

He nodded, "Yes I expect you're right my love, but then you always were," he added with that cheeky grin of his.

They looked down one last time.

"Ready?" He asked.

She nodded.

Then there was a strange whooshing sound and she was almost blinded by the bright white light that was surrounding them both. It felt like the light was love enveloping them in a warm embrace and she felt so very, very peaceful.

Cyril held her hand as they walked on through the light, "Come on lass," he said, "let's go home..."

Thank you for reading...and for supporting Alzheimer's Research

Glossary of Terms

1 **ITMA:** It's That Man Again Wartime comedy radio programme.

2 **Glad Rags**: Dressy clothes worn for social occasion.

3 **Not the full shilling**: Slang for mentally deficient.

4 **Dinky**: Toy cars dating from the 1950's.

5 **Loose Women**: Daytime British TV magazine programme.

6 **Flat:** British for Apartment.

7 **Double Diamond**: Brand of beer.

8 **Mrs Thatcher**: A tough British Prime Minister.

9 **The bee's knees:** Slang for someone who is excellent, a cut above the rest.

10 Lewis's: Large department store in Manchester

UK.

11 Donkey stone: A sort of scouring block used to

clean stone steps in Northern Mill towns.

12 Once every Preston Guild: Means infrequently,

like guild meetings, a Northern phrase.

.

Printed in Great Britain
by Amazon